For Rachel, Austin, and Tyler,
who are udderly adorable.
—CRS

For my five moootiful children.
I couldn't have written this
without your moooooods!
—KC

To Iñaki, for continuing to look
for a better moooood
—CR

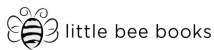 little bee books

251 Park Avenue South, New York, NY 10010
Text copyright © 2020 by Corey Rosen Schwartz and Kirsti Call
Illustrations copyright © 2020 by Claudia Ranucci
Manufactured in China LEO 0820
First Edition
10 9 8 7 6 5 4 3 2 1
Names: Schwartz, Corey Rosen, author. | Call, Kirsti, author. | Ranucci, Claudia, 1973- illustrator.
Title: Mootilda's bad mood / by Corey Rosen Schwartz and Kirsti Call; illustrated by Claudia Ranucci.
Description: First edition. | New York: Little Bee Books, [2020] | Audience: Ages 4-8. | Audience: Grades K-1.
Summary: Mootilda visits her friends Identifiers: LCCN 2020000417
Subjects: CYAC: Stories in rhyme. | Cows—Fiction. | Mood (Psychology)—Fiction. | Domestic animals—Fiction.
Classification: LCC PZ8.3.S29746 Mo 2020 | DDC [E]—dc23 LC record available at https://lccn.loc.gov/2020000417
ISBN: 978-1-4998-1086-8
littlebeebooks.com

For more information about special discounts on bulk purchases,
please contact Little Bee Books at sales@littlebeebooks.com.

MOOTILDA'S
BAD MOOD

by Corey Rosen Schwartz and Kirsti Call   illustrated by Claudia Ranucci

Mootilda woke up in a huff
with hay stuck in her hair.
"What's going on? My pillow's gone.
My doll's way over there!"

She hugged her moomaw cow who said,
"Oh sweetie, have a treat."
She grabbed the stick and took a lick.
It landed at her feet.

"I'm in a ba

Her moomaw said, "That's terri-bull,
but don't stay in and mope."
She smoothed her cowlick, smooched her cheek,
and said, "Go jump some rope!"

Some calves were playing double Dutch.
Mootilda caught some air.
She skipped and tripped, a bucket tipped,
and milk spilled everywhere!

"I'm in a bad MOOOD!"

"Hay hay there now, don't have a cow!
We'll get this mess remoooved.
A sooothing swim will cool you down.
Your moood will soon improoove!"

Some lambs were diving in the pond.
They lunged and plunged—*kerplop*.
Mootilda leapt, but whack, went *SMACK*!
A bovine belly flop!

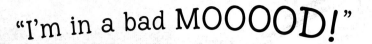

Some pigs were riding bicycles.
Mootilda grabbed a spare.
They squealed and wheeled; she meant to yield
but flew up in the air!

"I'm in a bad MOOOOOD!

This morning stinks. I think I'm jinxed!
I'm scraped up from that fall."

"You're fine, don't whine," replied the swine.
"That's hogwash. Play some ball!"

Some ponies dribbled, shot, and scored.
Mootilda dunked and dashed.
She alley-ooped but missed the hoop.
The ball bounced off and crashed!

"I'm in a bad MOOOOOOD!

This day's been a COW-tastrophe!
I think I've got a curse."

The chickens clucked. "You've got bad luck?
Our day's been even worse!"

"Our stuff was pecked. Our projects wrecked.
We're feeling bleak and blue."

"Oh my, what a COW-incidence!
You're in a bad mood too?"

"We're in a ba

Mootilda took a breath and said,
"I don't know who's upsetter!
Let's huddle and COW-miserate
and then we'll feel much better."

Mootilda cheered the chickens up
with creamy cold dessert.
Just then, a crow flew way too low
and knocked hers in the dirt!

Mootilda gasped!

And then she laughed.
Her laughs rang on and on.
Then suddenly, to her surprise,
her glooomy mood was . . . gone!

Mootilda felt **moog-nificent.**
She'd really changed her tune.
"My **melan-cow-ly** mood has left.
I'm NOW over the MOOOOOOOOOOOOON!"

"I'm in a bad mood."